Shadowcut Press
5325 Radford Ave.
Valley Village, CA 91607

Shakespeare's Oz

Shakespeare's Oz

Shakespeare's

DRAMATIS PERSONAE

DOROTHY
TOTO, a dog
PROFESSOR/OZ
GLINDA
WITCH
SCARECROW
PEWTER MAN
LION
NIKKO servant to the WITCH
GUARD of Emerald City gates
WINKIES guards to the WITCH
EM, aunt to DOROTHY
OWEN, uncle to DOROTHY
BOATSWAIN
CHORUS

Shakespeare's Oz

Shakespeare's OZ

ACT I

ACT 1 scene 1

Ship's hull
Enter CHORUS (The PROFESSOR)

CHORUS
Oh, for a muse of fire that would ascend
The brightest heaven of invention!
A kingdom for a stage, witches to act,
And monarchs to behold the swelling scene!
But pardon, gentles all,
The flat unraisèd spirits that hath dared
On this unworthy scaffold to bring forth
So great an object. Can this cockpit hold
The vasty fields of Oz?
Suppose within the girdle of these walls
Are now confined two mighty monarchies
Whose high uprearèd and abutting fronts
The perilous wide ocean parts asunder.
Think, when we talk of lions, that you see them
Printing their proud paws i' th' receiving earth,
For 'tis your thoughts that now must deck our lass
Carry her here and there, jumping o'er times,
Turning th' accomplishment of many days
Into an hour-glass;
Five score and nineteen years hath our tale givn'
Faithful service to the youthful spirit.
And Time no power o're its goodly word.
To thee whose faith hath givn' in return
Admit me chorus to this history;
Who, prologue-like, your humble patience pray
Gently to hear, kindly to judge our play.

Exit CHORUS

Enter DOROTHY with TOTO

DOROTHY
(Sings)
Somewhere o're yonder rainbow
Sparrows fly,
Birds fly o're yonder rainbow
Wherefore then why can't I?

PROFESSOR
Break off thy song, and haste thee quick away.

DOROTHY
I cry you mercy, sir,
Though music oft hath such a charm
To make bad good.

PROFESSOR
Believe me so,
My mirth it much displeased, but pleased my woe.
Say, what manner of traveler art thou?
Well, well, conceal yourself amongst the crew eh? And whom
might you be?
Nay—tell me not. Thou art traveling disguised. Nay. Tis a
falsehood.
Self imposed exile?

DOROTHY
How didst thou guess?

PROFESSOR
Not a guess but an affirmation!
Now, wherefore do you run away?

DOROTHY
Wherefore --

PROFESSOR
Tell me not.
Your...uncle did murder thy father and has taken your mother
as wife?
Nay. Speak not.
They respect you not back home and you wish to see distant
lands across the sea
But be patient, for the world is broad and wide.

DOROTHY
A man is master of his liberty;
Time is their master, and when they see time
They'll go or come. Wherefore should their liberty than mine be
more?

PROFESSOR
Yes --

DOROTHY
Prithee sir, can we go along with thee?

Toto bites fish off skewer

DOROTHY o.s.
Toto, nay! We he has not bid us eat.

PROFESSOR
He is welcome. As one beast to
another, eh? Now to the matter.
You wish to hoist sail for home?

DOROTHY
Nay, I wish to go along with you.
For they care about me not at home.
I have set up my rest to run away, so
I will not rest till I have run some ground.

PROFESSOR
Come now...

DOROTHY
Nay, I'll be sworn
I have sat in the stocks for puddings Toto hath stolen,
otherwise he had been executed.
I have stood on the pillory for geese he hath killed, otherwise he
had suffered for 't.
I beg thee, sirrah, tell them not we hide here beneath decks?

PROFESSOR
Prithee, sit.
This be the same crystal used by Priests of Egypt
And fortold that Charmian would outlive the lady
Whom she served.
The undiscovered country from whom no traveler returns
But this crystal can messenger twixt both realms be.
Now my child, shut thine eyes,
In nature's infinite book of secrecy
A little I can read.

*Professor removes portrait from DOROTHY's purse. Studies it,
then replaces.*

DOROTHY
Good sir, give me good fortune.

A Soothsayer Listening to Sounds of the Mountains
"On the Art of Prophecy," from Olaus Magnus' History of the Nordic Peoples, 1555.

PROFESSOR
I make not, but foresee.
Now open thine eyes and we shall together gaze.
What be this? A cottage and barn, with wall of stone

DOROTHY
That be our slobbery farm!

PROFESSOR
Ay, verily!

PROFESSOR
There be a spinster in poor petticoat
And aged wrinkles on her brow.

DOROTHY
Ay, that be Aunt Em.

PROFESSOR
Emily be her name.

DOROTHY
'Tis true. What does she?

PROFESSOR
Wherefore , she weeps.

DOROTHY
Oh --

PROFESSOR
Someone hath done her wrong.
Someone hath crack'd her heart.

DOROTHY
Be it I?

PROFESSOR
'Tis someone she loves entirely and has shown kindness to.
Someone she hath provided for in sickness.

DOROTHY
Had I the plague once. And she did play nursemaid till my heath returned.
What does she now?

PROFESSOR
She faints!

DOROTHY
Alack!

PROFESSOR
Like a brief candle, has the crystal gone dark. The rest is silence.

DOROTHY
Suppose she indeed be ill? Oh, I must sail home anon!

PROFESSOR
What, all so soon? Methought you desired to go with me
On this journey.

DOROTHY (picking up Toto)
Nay, I must implore the master to lay her a-hold,
And set her two courses off to home!
Grammercie good sir!

Thunder

BOATSWAIN (o.s.)
Heigh, my hearts! Yare! Yare!
Take in the topsail.—Tend to th' master's whistle.—
Blow, till thou burst thy wind, if room enough!

PROFESSOR
I pray now, keep below
Till the storm hath passed.
What cares these roarers for the name of Dorothy?

Thunder. DOROTHY *hits her head, falling unconscious. TOTO barks.*

BOATSWAIN (o.s.)
Mercy on us!—We split, we split!

PROFESSOR
Now would I give a thousand furlongs of sea
For an acre of barren ground: long heath, brown furze,
anything.
The wills above be done, but I would fain die a dry death.

Woodcut depicting the shipwreck of São Bento. Boa Esperança. 1554

ACT 1 scene 2

The Coast of Oz

DOROTHY awakes

14

DOROTHY
Toto – I do suspect we be not in Sussex any longer.
O'r the rainbow we must be!

Enter GLINDA

DOROTHY
Now I know we be not in Sussex.
To GLINDA
What country, friend, is this?

GLINDA
This be OZ my lady.

DOROTHY
And what should I do in Oz?
The crew, they are in Elysium.
Perchance they be not drown'd.—What think you, madam?

GLINDA
It is perchance that you yourself were saved.
Be you an honest witch, or one most wicked
That can cheat on death?

DOROTHY
Be I not a witch
Thy name is Dorothy Gale from Sussex called.
(Aside)
Were such things here as I do speak about?
Or hath I eaten on the insane root
That takes the reason prisoner?

GLINDA *(motions to Toto)*

15

Well, come, be that the witch?

DOROTHY
This be Toto, my dog.

GLINDA
I do admit I am vexed.
For the Munchkins did call upon me that a usurping witch
Had a bark from heaven dropped upon the Witch most Wicked
of the East.
And there be the bark, and here you be, and 'tis all that remains
of the Eastern hag.
Therefore, what the Munchkins wish to know is
Art thou a goodly witch or one most wicked in her ways?

DOROTHY
In honest plainness, I am most certainly a maid.
Witches are foul and ugly.
Laughter (o.s.)
Hark, what was that?

GLINDA
The Munchkins. They laugh for I am a witch.
I be Glinda, the Witch of the Northern Winds.

DOROTHY *(curtsying)*
I cry you mercy.
I never yet did hear of a fair witch.

GLINDA
Only witches whose souls are foul be ugly.
The Munchkins be pleased you have released the bondage that
the
Witch most Wicked of the Eastern Winds had upon them.

For the motions of her spirit were as dull as night
And her affections dark as Erebus.

DOROTHY
As strange unto your town as to your talk,
Who, every word by all my wit being scanned,
Want wit in all one word to understand.
Who be these Munchkins?

GLINDA
They are the native people of this land.
All tongues speak of thee, and the bleared sights
Are spectacled to see thee: your prattling nurse
Into a rapture lets her baby cry
While she chats thee: the kitchen malkin pins
Her richest lockram 'bout her reechy neck,
Clambering the walls to eye thee: stalls, bulks, windows,
Are smother'd up, leads fill'd, and ridges horsed
With variable complexions, all agreeing
In earnestness to see thee.
Calling out
Reveal thyselves and give her thanks.
Singing
Come hither from the furrow and be merry.
Make holiday. Your rye-straw hats put on,

Enter MUNCHKINS, giving flowers and gifts to DOROTHY

GLINDA
(sings)
'Twas hurled from the sea and she fell very far.
And Sussex she claims be the name of her star.

MUNCHKINS

(sing)
Sussex she claims be the name of her star.

(sings)
Honor, riches, marriage, blessing,
Long continuance, and increasing,
Hourly joys be still upon you.
Munchkins sing their blessings on you.

Earth's increase, foison plenty,
Barns and garners never empty,
Vines and clustering bunches growing,
Plants with goodly burden bowing—
Spring now comes to us at farthest
In the very end of harvest.
Scarcity and want shall shun you.
Munchkins' blessing so is on you.

(A trio of Munchkins approaches)
MUNCHKIN TRIO (sings)
We three embody The Guild of Saint Lolly
The Guild of Saint Lolly
A hey, Nonny, Nonny!
And in the name of the Guild of Saint Lolly
We wish to welcome thee to Munchkin Land

DOROTHY (aside)
If in England, I should report this now, would they believe me?
If I should say, I saw such natives—
For, certes, these are people of this land—
Who, though they are small in size, yet note,
Their manners are more gentle-kind than of
Our human generation you shall find
Many—nay, almost any.

Enter WITCH

DOROTHY
Methought you pronounced her death?

GLINDA
T'was her sister -- the Witch most Wicked of
the Eastern wind. This be Sycorax, the foul Witch of the
Western wind, who with age and envy has grown into a hoop.
For mischiefs manifold and Sorceries terrible
To enter human hearing, she be far worse than her sibling.

WITCH
Let me see her. Out, alas! She's cold.
Her blood is settled, and her joints are stiff.
Death, that hath ta'en her hence to make me wail,
Ties up my tongue and will not let me speak.

GLINDA
You should hear reason.

WITCH
And when I have heard it, what blessing brings it?

GLINDA
If not a present remedy, at least a patient
sufferance.

WITCH
I cannot hide what I am:
I must be sad when I have cause and smile
At no man's jests. Though I cannot be said to

Be a flattering honest witch, it must not be denied
But I am a plain-dealing villain.

GLINDA
Then wash your sister from the earth with thy tears and be
done with it.

WITCH
Weep'st not so much for her death,
As that the villain lives which slaughtered her.
(to DOROTHY)
'Twas it you did this deed?

GLINDA
Leave her be, witch!

WITCH
Stay behind this business! I shall be revenged!
(to DOROTHY)
You have the look of guilt upon thy face,
These nails should rend that beauty from your cheeks.

DOROTHY
Nay! Be this an accident!

WITCH
If I thought that, I tell thee, homicide,
These nails should rend that beauty from your cheeks.

GLINDA
Do not you remember the slippers adorned withal crimson?

WITCH

The slippers -- yes.....the slippers!

The Witch of the East's legs protruding from underneath the shipwreck, the crimson slippers disappear and the stockings are drawn back under the sand

WITCH
The slippers crimson red. What hath thou done with them?
Hand them o'er!

GLINDA *(motioning to DOROTHY)*
You are come too late! There they are, and there shall stay!

DOROTHY
Oh!

WITCH
Return them thus! They be of no use to thee
For I alone know their hidden charms.

GLINDA
Stay thy ground.
For their magic will prove powerful indeed as her need for
them is great.

WITCH
Stay behind this business, or a pox on thee!

GLINDA
(laughs)
What stuff! You hath no power here.
Avaunt, and quit my sight! Lest a bark be dropped upon thy foul
head.

WITCH
'Tis well. I shall bide my time and
For thee, fond girl,
Though full of our displeasure, yet we free thee
From the dead blow of it.
I'll shall be revenged my dainty, and thy cur!
What horrors lay in wait when plots astir.

Exit WITCH in cloud of fire and smoke

English witches and their familiars. (From "The Wonderful Discoverie of the Witches of Margaret and Phillip Flower," 1619.)
GLINDA
'Tis all well, she is gone.
Pooh! It smells to heaven this Sulphur!

Methinks thou hast an enemy made of the witch of Western
Wind.
O lady, fly this place,
Intelligence is given where you are hid.

DOROTHY
I would not for the world then passage back,
But what be the way to Sussex from here?
For unless there be a ship hoisting sail,
I cannot return by how I came.

GLINDA
Nay, 'tis true. Only the most wonderful
Wizard of Oz may know.

DOROTHY
The Wizard of Oz? Be he kind or wicked?

GLINDA
A goodly sorcerer but strange as well
In far off Emerald City doth he dwell.
Importune his help to send thee straight home.
Did'st thou bring thy broomstaff from ocean foam?

DOROTHY
Nay my lady

GLINDA
Well on feet must you travel very far
Will you be ruled by me as guiding star?

DOROTHY
Ay, madam.
So you will not o'errule me to my death.

GLINDA
To thine own peace.

DOROTHY
And where does one begin?

GLINDA
Just follow the path of Golden Brick
The Munchkins shall see thee to the border.
And this above all else: to thine own feet must the slippers stay
Or you shall be the witch's prey.

MUNCHKINS
Singing
Just follow the path of golden brick
And do not let the clock a tic...

DOROTHY *(aside)*
What relish is in this? How runs the stream?
Or I am mad, or else this is a dream.
Let fancy still my sense in Lethe steep;
If it be thus to dream, still let me sleep!

(Exeunt)

Shakespeare's OZ

---∞---

ACT II

ACT 2 scene 1

A Crossroads
Enter DOROTHY with TOTO. A SCARECROW stands nearby

DOROTHY
There's not a man I meet but doth salute me
As if I were their well-acquainted friend;
Some tender money to me; some invite me;
Some other give me thanks for kindnesses;
Some offer me commodities to buy:
Even now a tailor call'd me in his shop
And show'd me silks that he had bought for me.
Sure, these are but imaginary wiles
And New World sorcerers inhabit here.
(beat)
Follow the path of golden brick
Which way go we now?

SCARECROW (pointing)
'Tis a very pleasant path.

DOROTHY
Who speaks?
Do not jest, Toto, Scarecrows speaketh not.

SCARECROW
And this way be pleasant too.

DOROTHY
'Tis strange. Was he not pointing the contrary?

SCARECROW
I warrant, some go both ways.

DOROTHY
Wherefore, you spoke!
Aside
A living drollery! Now I will believe
That there are unicorns!

SCARECROW shakes his head, then nods

DOROTHY
Do you that on purpose, or canst thou decide?

SCARECROW
There's the rub!
I hast no more brain than I have in mine elbows;

DOROTHY
How can you speak if brain you are without?

SCARECROW
I know not. And yet there are those with brains without that talk much,
Would'st thou agree?

DOROTHY
Verily.
Well, how fares thee sirrah?

SCARECROW
How fares thee madam?

DOROTHY
Happily met.

SCARECROW

27

By my troth, I am not well in health.
'Tis a tedious thing to be here perched
With pike up thy back
When day's oppression is not eased by night
But day by night and night by day oppressed.

DOROTHY
Oh, misery! A discomfort indeed.
And canst thou free thyself?

SCARECROW
Nay, you see I am quite stuck.

DOROTHY
Let me aide thee.

SCARECROW
That is very kind, madam, I thank thee.

He falls and she helps him up

DOROTHY
Feel your legs? You stand.

SCARECROW
Oh, it is good to be free of that stake!
Did I frighten thee?

DOROTHY
Heavens, no.

SCARECROW
Methought not.

The Scarecrow. Illustration by Jordan Monsell

Enter crow
SCARECROW
They do laugh at me.
'Twas set up to fear the birds of prey,

And let it keep one shape, till custom make it
Their perch and not their terror.
And this half shirt is but two napkins tacked together and
thrown over my shoulders like a herald's coat without sleeves;
and the shirt, to say the truth, stolen from the red-nose
innkeeper of Winkieland.
A failure am I, for have I not a brain.
My head is as concave as a covered goblet or a worm-eaten nut.

DOROTHY
How came you upon this field?

SCARECEOW
I was born but two days prior. First the Munchkin farmer did
paint two eyes so that I may see.
Then two ears so that I may hear. A nose so that I may smell.
And finally lips so that I may speak.
And yet his brush could not paint a brain.

DOROTHY
What would ye do with this brain?

SCARECROW
I would sit upon the ground and tell sad stories of the death of
kings.
Laugh at gilded butterflies, and hear poor rogues
Talk of court news, and I would talk with them too—
Who loses and who wins, who's in, who's out—
And take upon 's the mystery of things
As if I were God's spy.

He spins around

DOROTHY

O Wonderful, most wonderful!
Wherefore , if our Scarecrow back in
Sussex could do as you do, would the crows
Lose their feathers!

SCARECROW
Be this true?

DOROTHY
Verily

SCARECROW
And where be this Sussex?

DOROTHY
It be my home, across the sea.
I wish nothing more than to return,
So I travel straightforth to the City of Emeralds to bid the wizard
there to help.

SCARECROW
You travel to see the wizard?

DOROTHY
Ay.

SCARECROW
Think it possible this wizard could conjure me a brain?

DOROTHY
I cannot say.
But if not, you shall be no worse off than thou art at present.

SCARECROW

You advise me well.

DOROTHY
In the sincerity of honest kindness.
Though treacherous this journey be
As I have a witch who wishes me dead.

SCARECROW
I be not afeard of any witch.
I be not afeard of most anything,
Mayhaps the flame.

DOROTHY
Of which I blame thee not

SCARECROW
When a man's verses cannot be understood nor a man's
Good wit seconded with the forward child, understanding,
It strikes a man more dead than a great reckoning in a little
room.
Truly, I would the farmer had made me poetical.

DOROTHY
You are marvelous merry, sir. Will you go with me?

SCARECROW
Indeed I shall, my lady

DOROTHY
Then we shall set forth

Exeunt

ACT 2 scene 2
Enter DOROTHY, TOTO, and SCARECROW

DOROTHY picks an apple from a tree

DOROTHY
Methought the wood began to move.

TREE
What dost thou?

DOROTHY
We have traveled far and hunger overtakes....didst thou speak?

TREE
Hear thee? She hungers!
She dies that touches any of this fruit.

DOROTHY
O, heavens, I forget once 'gain that Sussex this is not.

SCARECROW
Make haste friend, you would not wish those crabs. Hmph!

TREE
What means you thus? Those crabs? Do you say the fruit
I bear be not suitable?

SCARECROW

Nay, but that she cares not for the burrowing worm

TREE
You....dare!

SCARECROW (to DOROTHY)
I'll show thee how to fetch apples.

TREE
Oh, I'll give thee burrowing worms!

throws apples

SCARECROW
Help thyself.
And I pray thee, sort thy heart to patience;
These few days' wonder will be quickly worn.

Dorothy chases a rolling apple to the feet of the PEWTER MAN.
She picks up the oil can.

DOROTHY
Wherefore , it be a man! A man of pewter!

SCARECROW
No longer shall you gaze on't, lest your fancy
May think anon it moves.

DOROTHY
Let be, Let be. What was he that did make it? See, good cuz,
Would you not deem it breathed? And that those veins
Did verily bear blood?

SCARECROW

Masterly done:
The very life seems warm upon his lip.

DOROTHY
The fixture of his eye has motion in't,
As we are mock'd with art.

PEWTER MAN
Pot of oil....pot of oil....

DOROTHY
Live you? Or are you aught
That man may question? You seem to understand me.

PEWTER MAN
Pot of oil....

SCARECROW
Oil say you?

DOROTHY
Pot of oil? Ah, here.
Where shall I oil thee first?

PEWTER MAN
Twixt my lips.

SCARECROW
His mouth.

She oils him

PEWTER MAN
By the gods, I can freely speak!

Time hath not yet so dried this blood of mine
Nor age so eat up my invention.
Prithee, my elbows and knees?

DOROTHY
Art thou hurt?

PEWTER MAN
Nay, this unlooked-for life comes well.
For I have held that axe a great while.

Woodcutter. 1493

The Pewter Man. Illustration by Jordan Monsell

DOROTHY
Good faith, how came these things to pass?

PEWTER MAN
One Nicholas Chopper was I in life
And loved the lady Anne of Munchkinland
A servant of the Wicked Western Witch.
Felled the trees of Oz dids't I till that day
Was Cursed by that most foul witch Sycorax
Who, green with envy did bewitch my axe
Which with swift work like wingèd mercury
Did part my limbs from my core.
Sans legs, sans hands, sans heart, sans everything.

DOROTHY
Sans heart ?

PEWTER MAN
Procured I the service of a smith whom
With his tools did make me a counterfeit
To replace each limb lost to cursed axe.
But beating heart within this empty chest.
'Twas two moons ago was I chopping wood
When skies above did turn the darkest pitch
Twist chop my armor did rust and stand I
Here in apoplexy till you came 'long.

A blacksmith

DOROTHY
Well now thou art perfect.

PEWTER MAN
Think me perfect? Knock upon my chest if think me perfect.
 Hollow as a drum. This rude form is but a cistern for foul toads.
(*He Sings*)

I'd befriend every sparrow
And Cupid with his arrow
If I had a beating heart.

DOROTHY

I never heard a better.

SCARECROW
Be the same. I shall bid the wizard for brains instead of a heart.
For a fool would not know what to do with a heart if he had one

PEWTER MAN
 I shall take the heart. For brains do not make one happy.
And happiness be the best thing in all the world.

DOROTHY
Will you accompany us to the City of Emerald good sir knight
And bid the Wizard for a heart?

PEWTER MAN
The City of Emerald?
Be it a treacherous journey.
Mayhap in thunder, lightning, or in rain.

SCARECROW
But say you most desire a heart.

DOROTHY
And I shall keep close the pot of oil.

PEWTER MAN
And if this wizard denies me a heart?

DOROTHY
But he must! For we have traveled long already.

Enter WITCH above

WITCH
Call that long? Wherefore , you have just begun!
Have you forgotten me of late?

SCARECROW
How now, you secret, black, and midnight hag?

WITCH
Giving the lady your charity, my fine gentles?
Well stand all aloof
(To SCARECROW)
Or I shall stuff pillows with thee!
Why you be so lean that blasts of January
Would blow you through and through.
(To PEWTER MAN)
And thou shalt be pinched
As thick as honeycomb, each pinch more stinging
Than bees that made 'em.
(To SCARECROW)
Crowkeeper! Wish you to play at bowls?

Throws down a ball of fire at them

(To DOROTHY)
And as for thee, my cherubim
As wicked dew as e'er my mother brushed
With raven's feather from unwholesome fen
Drop on thee! A southwest blow on ye
And blister you all o'er!
You all know, security
Is mortals' chiefest enemy.

Exit WITCH in cloud of smoke

41

SCARECROW
I be not afeard of her.
Had I a brain, more busy than the labouring spider would it be;
Weaving tedious snares to trap mine enemies.
I'll see thee safely to the Wizard.

PEWTER MAN
And I, my lady. I shall see thee reach the Wizard,
Whether I get a heart or nay.

DOROTHY
Nay, I beg thee, remain here or harm
Will befall you both.

SCARECROW
Think you we shall idly stand looking on
Allow this witch to conjure fire?
Well we shall turn her balls to gun-stones
And her soul shall stand sore charged for
The wasteful vengeance that shall fly with her.

DOROTHY
Thou are the best friends. We are well met now.
Our hands are full of business. Let's away.
Advantage feeds him fat while men delay.

Exeunt

ACT 2, scene 3

Another part of the Forest
Enter DOROTHY, TOTO, SC ARECROW and PEWTER MAN

DOROTHY
I do not like this place

SCARECROW
I know not, but methinks it shall grow darker before the light
returns.

DOROTHY
Think you we shall meet wild beasts?

PEWTER MAN
We may

SCARECROW
Beasts that eat straw?

PEWTER MAN
Aye-- but mostly tigers, lions, wolves, and bears.

DOROTHY
In such a place as this
Did Thisbe fearfully o'erstrip the dew
And saw the lion's shadow ere himself
And ran dismayed away.

SCARECROW
Lions?

PEWTER MAN
And tigers, bears, and wolves.

DOROTHY
O my!
A wilderness of beasts? Tigers must prey, and Oz affords no prey
But me and mine.

Sound of growling

DOROTHY
O heavens! What manner of beast is this?

Enter LION

SCARECROW
I shall shield thee! For a lion among ladies is a most dreadful thing.
There is not a more fearful wildfowl than your lion living. And we ought to look to 't.

LION
I challenge thee! Look to thyselves!
Whom be the first? Betake you to your guard! Betake your guard!
I'll fight thee with one paw bound. I'll fight thee on one leg
Or like Cupid hoodwinked with a scarf.
What villain? An ax?
(snarls)

PEWTER MAN
Prithee, get thee gone and let us alone!

LION
Oh, art thou afeard? I am not yet well breathed!
Dismount thy tuck, be yare in thy preparation
Come at thee, thou uneven bale of hay.

SCARECROW
So vulgarly and personally accused, Lion.

PEWTER MAN
I have heard of some kind of men that put
Quarrels purposely on others, to taste their valor.
Belike this is a beast of that quirk.

LION starts at TOTO. DOROTHY strikes LION

DOROTHY
For shame!

LION *(weeping)*
Wherefore strike me so? I did not devour him.

DOROTHY
Nay, but was your intent.

Would you hurt an offenseless dog to affright us?
So blunt thou the lion's paws,
Pluck the keen teeth from the fierce lion's jaws,

LION
If you were civil and knew courtesy,
You would not do me thus much injury.
If you strike us, do we not bleed?
O, let her not come near me!

DOROTHY
Good heavens, here's such a coil.
Why, thou art a coward

LION
'Tis an honest truth, in faith, I be a coward.
Afraid of myself even.
Sleep hath escaped me in many moons.

PEWTER MAN
Dids't thou attempt a counting sheep?

LION
'Tis no good for I be afeard of them.

SCARECROW
Alas. Think ye the wizard could help him?

DOROTHY
Why not? Attend us Lion?
We be on a journey to see the wizard. To bid him a heart.

PEWTER MAN
And he a brain.

DOROTHY
And courage for thee.

LION
Unworthy as I am, to follow you?
You show me unlooked for kindness.
My life has been insupportable!
Creeping in this petty pace from day to day
To the last syllable of recorded time.

DOROTHY
Oh. Speak you so gently? Pardon me, I pray you:
I thought that all things had been savage here;
And therefore put I on the countenance
Of stern commandment. But whate'er you are
That in this wood inaccessible,
Under the shade of melancholy boughs,
Lose and neglect the creeping hours of time
If ever you have look'd on better days,
If ever from your eyelids wiped a tear
And know what 'tis to pity and be pitied,
Let gentleness my strong enforcement be:
In the which hope I blush, and hide my sword.
Are you native of this place?

LION
Aye madam

DOROTHY
Your accent is something finer than you could purchase in so
removed a dwelling.

LION

I have been told so of many. Indeed a mad philosopher taught
me to speak.
But teach me not the art of bravery.

DOROTHY
I do wonder if this mad philosopher you speak of be the same
Wizard we seek. Come. Let us be off to see this Magician of Oz
Because of the wonders they claim he does.

Exeunt

ACT 2, scene 4
Enter WITCH

WITCH
Double, double, toil and trouble
Fire burn, and cauldron bubble
Eye of newt and toe of frog
Wool of bat and tongue of dog
Yet something soothing to the smell
Like poppy flowers 'pon the dell
Something now to make them sleep.
In the cauldron they do steep   (*Exeunt*)

Witches with cauldron

ACT 2, scene 5

A field outside the Emerald City
Enter DOROTHY, TOTO, SCARECROW, PEWTER MAN, and LION

DOROTHY
At last, though long, The City of Emeralds draws on apace!
A most wonderful wizard must he be that lives in such a palace.

LION
Come on, away my fellows!

SCARECROW
Let us be swift!

DOROTHY
Let us run!

SCARECROW
The City of Emeralds!

DOROTHY
I...I can fly no further.

SCARECROW
Here -- give us thy hands, and we shall pull thee.

DOROTHY
Nay, Faintness constraineth me
To measure out my length on this flowery bed.

She falls asleep

Extracting raw opium from a poppy seed pod. France. 1614

SCARECROW
Oh, you can't rest now -- we're nearly there!

LION
What did she -- do that for?

SCARECROW
Dorothy!

PEWTER MAN
Good lady, sleep no more!

LION

Dorothy!

Enter WITCH (unseen)

WITCH
Thy cries fall upon deaf ears!
(laughs)
Fair is foul, and foul is fair
Hover through the fog and filthy air.

WITCH *Exits*

PEWTER MAN
(crying)
Oh - oh, poor Dorothy!

SCARECROW
Hold thy tears or rust thyself once 'gain!

LION
Yawning
Oh, I am exceeding weary .

SCARECROW
Don't you start it, too!

PEWTER MAN
Bear her 'pon our shoulders?

SCARECROW
Verily, should we try.

PEWTER MAN
Oh -- now look at him! This is terrible!

SCARECROW
Here, PEWTER MAN -- help me.

SCARECROW
Oh, heavy deed!
She budge not. An this be a
Charm, I doubt it not!

PEWTER MAN
'Tis the Witch most Wicked! What shall we do?
What, ho? Help!

SCARECROW
Peace, cease thy shrieking
For no one hears thee.
(Beat)
Help! Help!

Enter GLINDA waving her wand over the field.

SCARECROW
Look! How it snows!
It melts away her sleep in water-drops!
She wakes!

DOROTHY
This land acquaints a woman with strange bedfellows!

LION
'Tis weather most strange!

DOROTHY (to PEWTER MAN)

Look! He has rust again. Oh, give me the
Pot of oil. Why do you weep Sir Knight?

PEWTER MAN
In sooth, I know not why I am so sad.
But stuff 'tis made of, with lack of heart,
I am to learn.

DOROTHY
The Emerald City is within our grasp,
Excitement fills me, take these hands to grasp.

Exeunt

Shakespeare's OZ

ACT III

ACT 3 scene 1

Witch's Castle
Enter WITCH

WITCH
A curse 'pon it! This girl be ever aided.
Yet shoe or shoeless my power be great
And woe to those who tempt a witch's fate.
(Grabs broomstaff)
To the Emerald City I shall fly
Fair is foul, and foul is fair
Hover through the fog and filthy air.

Exit WITCH

ACT 3 scene 2

Emerald City gates.
Enter DOROTHY, TOTO, LION, SCARECROW, and PEWTER MAN

VOICES
singing
Forebear thy breath
Forbear thy heart
Forbear they hope --
March to the gate
And bid it 'ope.

DOROTHY knocks.

Enter PORTER

PORTER
Who knocks?

DOROTHY AND OTHERS
We did.

PORTER
Whence come you? What's your will? And what shall I say you
are?

DOROTHY AND OTHERS
We would see the Wizard.

PORTER
Ooooh! The Wizard?
He takes not audience.

DOROTHY
If it please you sir, I needs must see the Wizard. The Goodly
Witch
Of the Northern Winds charged me and we are fortified against
any denial.

PORTER
What be thy proof?

SCARECROW
She adorns the crimson shoes that were besto'd upon her.

PORTER
Oh......so she is! Well, bust my buttons! Wherefore
didn't you say that in the.......first place?

DOROTHY
How is the Wizard esteemed here in the city?

PORTER
Of very reverend reputation, madam,
Of credit infinite, highly beloved,
Second to none that lives here in the city.
But to those that are dishonest, he is most terrible.
His word might bear my wealth at any time
And yet, few have lain eyes on him.

Enter WITCH above. All point.

DOROTHY
It be the Witch! She hath followed!

PEWTER MAN
She's fortified against any denial.

Witches flying, from Mathers' Wonders of the Invisible World (1689)

SCARECROW
S-u-r-r-e-n-d-e-r- Dorothy or face death!
SYCORAX.

PORTER
Oh, if ever you disturb our skies again
Your life shall pay the forfeit of the peace.
For this time all the rest depart away.
You Dorothy, shall go along with me.

To know our wizard's pleasure in this case.

CROWD
To the Wizard!
He shall explain all

Enter GUARD

GUARD
Peace! Look to yourselves! All's well. All's well.
The Great and Most Powerful Oz
Has matters in hand. Now get thee gone!

DOROTHY
If it you please you, sir. We wish to see the
Wizard anon.

GUARD
The Great Oz does not grant audience.

DOROTHY
But I beseech thee. 'Tis a matter most urgent.

GUARD
I wonder that you will still be talking, madam.
Nobody marks you.

SCARECROW
But this be Dorothy!

GUARD
The Witch's Dorothy? Well that be a great difference. I cry you
mercy.
Await you here – I shall announce thee presently.

Exit GUARD

SCARECROW
Did'st thou hear? He shall announce us presently.
Anon I'll have a brain!

PEWTER MAN
Why, methinks I can hear my proud heart swell!

DOROTHY
And I shall be home in time to sup!

LION
And I will roar, that I will do any man's heart good to hear me. I
will roar, that I will make the Wizard say, "Let him roar again.
Let him roar again."

SCARECROW
An you should do it too terribly, you would fright the citizens,
that they would shriek. And that were enough to hang us all.

PEWTER MAN
That would hang us, every mother's son.

LION
Then I will aggravate my voice so that I will roar you as gently
As any sucking dove. I will roar you an 'twere any nightingale.
For this sorcerer, whose gentle heart fears not
The smallest monstrous mouse that creeps on floor,
May now perchance both quake and tremble here,
When lion rough in wildest rage doth roar.
Then know that I, Brrr by name, am

A lion fell, nor else no lion's dam.
For if I should as lion come in strife
Into this place, 'twere pity on my life.

Enter GUARD

GUARD
Get thee home. It is the Wizard's decree you leave this place.

SCARECROW
Then stand at your door like a sheriff's post, and be the
supporter to a bench.
It appears we have traveled this distance—and all for nothing.

DOROTHY
Oh -- and so happy was I.
Methought home was in my reach.

PEWTER MAN
Oh, do not weep

DOROTHY
But have I not cause to weep?

PEWTER MAN
As good cause as one would desire.
Therefore weep. But we shall see thee to the Wizard.

SCARECROW
Aye, but how?

LION
Shall I roar?

SCARECROW
At whom?

LION
I know not.

DOROTHY
Aunt Em respected me as her only daughter.
A better Aunt was their not, and rejected I her love by running off.
The soothsayer said she fell ill and may be close to death.
They say the tongues of the dying
Enforce attention like deep harmony:
Where words are scare, they are seldom spent in vain,
For they breath truth that breath their words in pain.
She spoke my name and 'tis my fault that she lay ill.

GUARD begins to sob

DOROTHY
God, forgive me!

GUARD
Oh, lady, weep no more.
I shall escort thee to the Wizard
Thru this door.

Exeunt

ACT 3 scene 3
Throne Room
ENTER DOROTHY, TOTO, SCARECROW, LION, and PEWTER MAN

LION
Hold, good gentles, hold. I shall await they outside.

SCARECROW
What be the matter?

PEWTER MAN
He is fearful once 'gain.

DOROTHY
But the Wizard shall grant thee courage!

LION
Afeard am I to bid him for it.

DOROTHY
Then we shall bid him for you.

LION
'Tis all one. I shall await thee out there.

DOROTHY
For what reason I beseech you?

LION
For that I be afeard!

DOROTHY
Wouldst thou have that which thou
Esteem'st the ornament of life,
And live a coward in thine own esteem,
Letting "I dare not" wait upon "I would," like the poor cat I'th'
adage?

LION
OWW!!

SCARECROW
Why do you shout?

LION
Someone did my tail a'tug.

SCARECROW
That was thine own doing!
Now follow close by.

The head of OZ appears

OZ
Come forward!

LION
Behold! Look! Lo!
I dare not look on that
Which might appall the devil.

OZ'S VOICE
I be Oz, of the Great and Powerful!
Who art thou?

DOROTHY (aside)
Oh, it offends me to the soul to hear a robustious fellow tear a
passion to tatters, to very rags, to split the ears of the
groundlings, who for the most part are capable of nothing but
inexplicable dumb-shows and noise. Your forgiveness.
(to OZ)
If it please your grace, I be Dorothy the meek.

We have come to bid thee--

OZ'S VOICE
Peace!
I am not one in so skipping a dialogue. I know wherefore you came.
Come hither PEWTER MAN.

PEWTER MAN steps forward

PEWTER MAN
Oh, 'tis me!

OZ
Thou dare to ask a heart of me?
You dismal clangour heard from far,
You clinking collection of rubbish!

PEWTER MAN
Verily your grace.
Whilst wandering the path of golden brick, we band of merry--

OZ'S VOICE
Peace! Thou peevish sheep!

PEWTER MAN
Oh!

OZ'S VOICE
And thou, Scarecrow, have the soaring insolence to
bid a brain? You billowing bundle of cattle fodder!

SCARECROW
V-Verily my Liege...rather, my Lordship, rather...

My Wizardry!

OZ'S VOICE
Peace!

Scarecrow steps back

OZ'S VOICE
And thee, Lion!

LION *steps slowly forward*
He faints

DOROTHY (to WIZARD)
Have you no modesty, no maiden shame,
No touch of bashfulness? When on bended knee
Did beseech thee for help!

OZ'S VOICE
His discretion, I am sure, cannot carry his valor, for the goose
carries not the fox.
Now silence! The charitable Oz hath every purpose of
Granting thy requests.

Others help LION to his feet

LION
What say he?

OZ'S VOICE
But first, ye must prove yourselves worthy.
Fetch me the broomstaff of that damnèd witch
Whose mischiefs manifold and sorceries terrible
To enter human hearing,

That spoiled your summer fields and fruitful vines,
Swills your warm blood like wash, and makes her trough
In your embowelled bosoms—this foul swine
Is now even in the center of this isle,
Near to the Haunted Forest as we learn.
From Emerald thither is but one day's march.
In God's name, cheerly on, courageous friends,
To reap the harvest of perpetual peace
By this one bloody trial of sharp war.

PEWTER MAN
But my humble Lord, to do this deed would be to murder!

OZ'S VOICE
Fetch me her broomstaff and thou shalt live as freely as thy lord
To call his fortunes thine.
Get thee hence! God in thy good cause make thee prosperous!
Be swift like lightning in the execution, And let thy blows,
Doubly redoubled, Fall like amazing thunder on the casque
Of thy adverse pernicious enemy!

LION
But---what if we are the first slain?

OZ'S VOICE
Screw your courage to the sticking-place! Rouse up thy youthful
blood, be valiant, and live.
Now get thee gone!

Exeunt all but GUARD

GUARD (aside)
And this man is now become a god, and this Guard
A wretched creature and must bend his body
If the wizard carelessly but nod on him.
He had a fever when he was in Gillikin,
And when the fit was on him, I did mark
How he did shake. 'Tis true, this god did shake!
His coward lips did from their color fly,
And that same eye whose bend doth awe the world
Did lose his luster. I did hear him groan,
Ay, and that tongue of his that bade the Ozians
Mark him and write his speeches in their books—
"Alas," it cried, "give me some drink, Guard!,"
As a sick girl. Ye gods, it doth amaze me
A man of such a feeble temper should
So get the start of the majestic world
And bear the palm alone.

Exits

ACT 3 scene 4

Inside the Haunted Forest
Enter DOROTHY, TOTO, SCARECROW, PEWTER MAN, and LION

LION (reading sign)
"Cursed be he who enter here."
(growls)

PEWTER MAN
Prepare ye. For on enemy ground are we.

DOROTHY
All torment and trouble inhabits here.
Some heavenly power guide us
Out of this fearful country!

Enter WITCH unseen

WITCH (aside)

Upon the corner of the moon
There hangs a vap'rous drop profound.
I'll catch it ere it come to ground.
And that distilled by magic sleights
Shall raise such artificial sprites
As by the strength of their illusion
Shall draw him on to his confusion.

Exits

SCARECROW
Oy, did'st thou bear witness?
Hand me thus!
I believe the dead do walk these woods.

71

PEWTER MAN
Tush, tush. Spirits? Nay.

LION
Believe you not in spirits of the dead?
There are more things in heaven and earth that are dreamt of
in your philosophy my good woodsman.

PEWTER MAN
No. Wherefore only -- Oh –

He is tossed to the ground

DOROTHY
Oh! Oh, PEWTER MAN!

SCARECROW
Before my God, I might not this believe
Without the sensible and true avouch
Of mine own eyes. Art thou well?

LION
Oh, arise fair sun and shun the envious moon!
Believe I now in these apparitions!
Oh, I do believe! I do believe!

Exeunt

ACT 3 scene 5

Witch's Castle
ENTER WITCH with crystal

WITCH
(laughing)
You shall believe in more than this
Before the night is thru.

Enter NIKKO, a MONKEY GENERAL

NIKKO
All hail, great master! Grave madam, hail! I come
To answer thy best pleasure, be 't to fly,
To swim, to dive into the fire, to ride
On the curled clouds. To thy strong bidding, task
Nikko and all his quality.

WITCH
Take thy army henceforth to the
Haunted Forest, and retrieve the girl and her cur!
Do what you will with the others, but wish I her alive and
unharmed!
T'will give thee no harm, I grant thee.
Take heed of the crimson shoes, for I wish them above all else.
Now, fly! Fly! Bring me forth the girl and her shoes.
Go hence with diligence.

NIKKO
My queen, it shall be done.
For I am your fiendish wanderer of the night
That frights the maidens of the villagery
And mislead night-wanderers, laughing

At their harm.

He exits
WITCH
Feed not thy sovereign's foe, my gentle earth,
Nor with thy sweets comfort their ravenous sense;
But let thy spiders, that suck up thy venom,
And heavy-gaited toads lie in their way,
Doing annoyance to the treacherous feet
Which with usurping steps do trample thee.

Exits

Witch with her familiars (1579)

Shakespeare's *OZ*

ACT IV

ACT 4 scene 1

Haunted Forest
ENTER DOROTHY, TOTO, SCARECROW, PEWTER MAN, and LION
with NIKKO and WINGED MONKEY SOLDIERS in pursuit

PEWTER MAN
Get thee hence! Avaunt!

NIKKO
You fools, I and my fellows
Are ministers of fate. The elements
Of whom your axes are tempered may as well
Wound the loud winds or with bemocked-at stabs
Kill the still-closing waters as diminish
One dowl that's in my plume.
For I am that fiendish wanderer of the night
That frights the maidens of the villagery
And mislead night-wanderers, laughing
At their harm.

Winged Monkeys tear SCARECROW apart, exit with DOROTHY
and TOTO

SCARECROW
Ho, Help!

LION
Wherefore , I'll -- Foul! Foul!

SCARECROW
Help! Help!

PEWTER MAN
Oh! What happened here?

SCARECROW
Drawn and quartered. My parts scattered to the four winds.

PEWTER MAN
Aye that be you over yonder.
And there. And there.

SCARECROW
Cease thy prattle and assemble my parts
Needs must we take chase and rescue Dorothy!

PEWTER MAN
Oh, this puzzles the will.

LION
Hold, this is the left leg.
He is stigmatical in making, truly.

PEWTER MAN
Alas, poor Dorothy.

We may never see her like again.

SCARECROW
What manner of creatures were they, think you?
And to where did they fly?
A fine thing to unravel at such a time.

PEWTER MAN
Now, now, fret not.
The castle of this witch we will surprise.
No boasting like a fool.
This deed we'll do before this purpose cool.

Exeunt

ACT 4 scene 2

Witch's Castle
Enter WITCH with DOROTHY and TOTO

WITCH *(taking TOTO)*
What a kindly cur!
What unlooked for pleasure!
'Tis kind of thee to visit in my loneliness.

DOROTHY
What means you with my dog? Return him hither!

WITCH
Forbear awhile.
In very good time my pretty flower.

DOROTHY

I beg of thee, return my loyal dog?

WITCH
Where are my slippers?

DOROTHY
The Goodly Witch of the North bid me not to.

WITCH (*handing* TOTO to NIKKO)
'Tis very well. To the river throw the dog and drown him.

DOROTHY
Nay! I beg of thee! Take the shoes but return my dog.

WITCH
You are wise.
She reaches for the shoes and is shocked

WITCH
Curse ye!

DOROTHY
I beg thy mercy, 'twas not my fault.
Can my dog be returned to me?

WITCH
Nay! Fool, that I am!
Remembered not these slippers will ne're
Be removed as long as thou breath life.

DOROTHY
What will you do?

WITCH
(aside)
Wisely and slowly lest the spell be damaged.
They stumble that run fast.

Toto jumps out of basket and runs out the door

DOROTHY
Make haste, Toto!

WITCH
Apprehend him!

DOROTHY
Run, Toto, run!
He hath prevented you!

WITCH
O, 'tis a foul thing when a cur cannot keep himself in all companies!
For this, be sure, tonight thou shalt have cramps,
Side-stitches that shall pen thy breath up.

Witch turns over hour glass

WITCH
Mark you thus?
My charms crack not, my spirits obey, and time
Goes upright with his carriage.
Yet time be not on thy side.

WITCH Exits

DOROTHY

Some devils bid but the parings of one's nail, a rush, a hair,
A drop of blood, a pin, a nut, a cherrystone: but she, more
covetous, would have these shoes.
Be wise, Dorothy. An if you give them her, the devil will have
more power still.

Blackout

ACT 4 scene 3

Haunted Forest
Enter PEWTER MAN , LION, and SCARECROW

PEWTER MAN
Meddling monkeys.
Come now, this be the best without pin and thread.

SCARECROW
Fear me not. We needs must find Dorothy.

PEWTER MAN
But to search we know not where.
But look who comes here! It is Dorothy's faithful hound!

Enter TOTO

PEWTER MAN
Toto! From whence came you?

SCARECROW
See thee not? He hath come to lead us. Lead on good cur!

PEWTER MAN
I am strong-framed. This witch cannot prevail with me.

LION
I do hope I may bend up every spirit
To his full height.

PEWTER MAN
And that thy tail holds out.

Exeunt

ACT 4 scene 4

Outside Witch's Castle. Enter LION, SCARECROW,
and PEWTER MAN

DOROTHY
(singing O.S.)
Someday, I'll wake and rub mine eyes
And in that land beyond the skies
Shall find me...

LION
What be this place?

SCARECROW
That be the castle where the Witch resides
And Dorothy 'gainst her will is held inside.

PEWTER MAN

To think of her in that dark prison cell makes me weep.
(*cries*)

SCARECROW
Hold thy tears for we have not the oil.

LION
But look who comes here!

Enter WINKIES marching

PEWTER MAN, LION and SCARECROW *hide behind a rock.*

SCARECROW
A plan I have devised to stealth us in.
Though yet when a wise man gives thee better counsel, give me mine again:
I would have none but knaves follow it, since a fool gives it.

LION
'Tis well. The fool hath a plan.

SCARECROW
And you wilt lead us.

A Winkie guard

LION
Say again?

SCARECROW
Verily

LION
Thou know'st we work by wit and not by witchcraft,
And wit depends on dilatory time.
But 'tis very well. Into the breach shall I straight
For our Dorothy's sake,
But first, a favor of thee cousin?

84

SCARECROW AND PEWTER MAN
Aye?

LION
Persuade me otherwise.

SCARECROW
It lies much in your holding up.

LION
I prithee, stay a little.

SCARECROW
Pray you, tread softly, that the blind mole may not hear a foot fall.

Three WINKIES spot them, run behind rock. They fight.
PEWTER MAN, SCARECROW and LION enter from behind rock--
all
dressed in Winkie Guard uniform.

SCARECROW
 'Twas not my plan, but alas, we prevailed.

PEWTER MAN
Well fought, Lion.

SCARECROW
Aye cousin

PEWTER MAN
I know not what would have befallen us without thy teeth and claws.

LION
I thank thee but I am one that had rather go with sir priest than sir knight. I care not who knows so much of my mettle.

SCARECROW
Come – have I another plan.

LION
But we are unannounced. Shall we mind better manners?

PEWTER MAN
Coraggio, bully-monster, coraggio!

Enter WINKIES marching. PEWTER MAN, Lion and SCARECROW join the end of the line. Enter WITCH'S castle then break away.

PEWTER MAN
Where to?

SCARECROW
There!

They Exit after TOTO

ACT 4 scene 5
Witch's Castle – Tower Room
Enter DOROTHY

DOROTHY
Death is a fearful thing.
To die, and go we know not where;
To lie in cold obstruction and to rot;
This sensible warm motion to become
A kneaded clod, oh I am afeard dear Aunt.

AUNTIE EM *(voice coming from crystal)*
Dorothy—cans't thou hear me?
Where art thou?

DOROTHY
I be here, dear Aunt, in Oz.
In a prison cell am I held by a horrid witch
And desperately wish to break free
And return home to thee.
Oh, your visage grows faint,
Do not leave me Aunt, for I am dreadfully frightened.
Return, I beg thee!

WITCH (from crystal)
Aunt Em -- Aunt Em, prithee, return! I beg thee!
I'll give thee Aunt Em, my beauty.
(laughs)

DOROTHY (throwing the crystal ball)
Now Dorothy, will you sit alone and beweep your outcast state?
And trouble deaf heav'n with your bootless cries,
And look upon myself, and curse my fate,
Or shall I endeavor to escape this place?
For had I twenty times so many foes,
And each of them had twenty times their power,
All these could not procure me any scathe,
So long as I am loyal, true and crimeless.

(Beat)
A pleasant thought but also a falsehood
For this wretched hag intends to kill me.

Dorothy pulls a nail from the floor and picks the lock of the prison door.

Enter SCARECROW, TINMAN, and LION

LION
We did hazard life to rescue you from she
That would do thee harm.

DOR
My gentle Lion, I knew you would prove valiant!
I thank ye kind friends But I did rescue myself.
Haply I thought on thee, and of England, and then my state,
Like to the lark at break of day arising
From sullen earth, sings hymns at heaven's gate.

SCARECROW
I pray you all—dispatch!

Enter WINKIES followed by WITCH

WITCH
So soon you take your leave? Why our reveals only just begun!

LION
The *Mousetrap!*

PEWTER MAN
Roar Lion!

LION
'Twould do no good.

WITCH
Harm them not but let them ponder a spell.
Imagine thou what tortures lay in wait for thee?

Witch throws down hour glass

PEWTER MAN
Out, you green-sickness carrion!

LION
Brace thyselves!

WITCH
Ring-a-ring o' roses
A pocket filled with spears.
Did'st thou think you could out-fox me?

Witch holds broom up to a torch. It catches fire.

First thrash the corn, then after burn the straw.

She sets the SCARECROW ablaze

SCARECROW
Help, masters, help! Look how I burn! Put out the light!

Dorothy throwing water at Scarecrow -- some of it hits the Witch

WITCH

What hast thou done? Cold, cold, my girl!
O that this too too solid flesh would melt
O cursed, cursed slave! Whip me, ye devils,
From the possession of this heavenly sight!
What a world! Here is my journey's end.

She dies

Enter NIKKO

LEADER
She's....she is dead! Dead as a ducat. Thou hast killed her!

DOROTHY
Meant I not to murder. 'Twas the fire she set ablaze!

WINKIE LEADER
Liberty! Freedom! Tyranny is dead!
Run hence, proclaim, cry it about the streets.
The Witch Most Wicked at last is dead!

WINKIES
The Witch Most Wicked at last is dead!

WINKIE LEADER
Ay, every man away.
Dorothy shall lead, and we will grace her heels
With the most boldest and best hearts of Oz.

DOROTHY
Wherefore rejoice?
You are content in this?

WINKIE LEADER

Aye, a crusty batch of nature she was.
And ne're 'gain will she strikes us with her broom.

DOROTHY
The broom! May we be given it?

LEADER
If it please you thus.

DOROTHY
I thank thee humble sir. And now with
Utmost expedience go we to the City of Emerald
And proclaim The witch most wicked is dead!

WINKIE LEADER
The Witch Most Wicked is dead!

ALL
The Witch Most Wicked is dead!
Enter NIKKO

NIKKO
O, pardon me, thou melting piece of earth,
That I am meek and gentle with these butchers!
Thou art the ruin of the noblest witch
That ever lived in the tide of times.
A great spirit gone! Thus did I desire it.
(sings)
Merrily, merrily shall I live now
Under the blossom that hangs on the bough.

Exeunt

Shakespeare's Oz

Shakespeare's *OZ*

ACT V

ACT 5 scene 1

Emerald City – Throne Room of the WIZARD
CROWD can be heard cheering offstage
Enter Scarecrow, Dorothy, Lion and PEWTER MAN. *OZ appears.*

OZ'S VOICE
Do mine eyes deceive me?
Hast thou returned?

DOROTHY *steps forward, places broomstaff before OZ*

DOROTHY
Prithee sir, have we carried out the task
You did give us. Brought you the broomstaff of that vile Witch.
Her too solid flesh did melt into a dew.

OZ
And what seemed corporal
Melted, as breath into the wind. Ingenious.

DOROTHY
Aye. If it please your grace
We would you keep your bond.

OZ
Not so hot. I needs must think upon this.
Leave me and return upon the morrow.

DOROTHY
On the morrow? But wish I to return ere now.

PEWTER MAN
Thou has had time enough!

LION
Ay!

OZ
Arouse not the wrath of this sorcerer. I charged thee—
Return on the morrow!

DOROTHY
I would I had your bond, for I perceive
A weak bond holds you. I'll not trust your word.

OZ'S VOICE
Dare censure the Great Oz? You lowly creatures you!

DOROTHY
Respect to your great place! And let the devil
Be sometime honor'd for his burning throne!

Toto pulls back the curtain to reveal the Wizard at the controls of
the throne apparatus

OZ'S VOICE
Think thyselves happy to be granted audience on the morrow
and not twenty moons.
The Great .....uh.....Oz hath spoken!

DOROTHY
Who art thou?

Toto pulls back the curtain. Illustration by Jordan Monsell

OZ'S VOICE
Regard not the man behind the arras. Make haste or
Come between the dragon and his wrath! Oz hath spoken!

DOROTHY
Who art thou?

WIZARD
Well, I —I be the Great and Powerful
Wizard of Oz.

DOROTHY
Thee?

WIZARD
Ay, the very same.

DOROTHY
I believe thee not.

WIZARD
Nay, 'tis true. There be no other wizard present.

SCARECROW
You rogue!

WIZARD
'Tis my deserving, and I do entreat it.

LION
I must confess I know this man.
When thou arrived first
Thou strok'st me and made much of me, wouldst give me
Water with berries in 't, and teach me how
To name the bigger light, and how the less,
That burn by day and night. And then I loved thee
And showed thee all the qualities o' th' isle,

The fresh springs, brine pits, barren place and fertile.
Cursed be I that did so!

WIZARD
T'was I, and am guilty of this charge.

DOROTHY
But a man, proud man,
Dress'd in a little brief authority,
Most ignorant of what he's most assured,
His glassy essence, like an angry ape,
Plays such fantastic tricks before high heaven
As make the angels weep; who, with our spleens,
Would all themselves laugh mortal.

SCARECROW
O, to him, to him, wench! He will relent.

DOROTHY
Oh thou embossed rascal!
Art thou not ashamed?

WIZARD
Nay, I be a goodly man, but a poor magician.
They say best men are molded out of faults;
And, for the most, become much more the better
For being a little bad.

SCARECROW
The more pity that fools may not speak wisely
That wise men do foolishly.

LION
Remember first to possess his books, for without them

He's but a sot, as I am, nor hath not
One spirit to command.

WIZARD
And therefore this rough magic
I here abjure,
I'll break my staff,
Bury it certain fathoms in the earth,
And deeper than did ever plummet sound
I'll drown my book.

SCARECROW
Before you do so, kindly send this lady back to England.

WIZARD
Prithee, thou see'st I have more flesh than another man
And therefore more frailty.

SCARECROW
And what of us?
What of the heart you promised this knight?

WIZARD
Well, I —

DOROTHY
Gratify these gentlemen,
For in my mind you are much bound to them.

SCARECROW
-- And the courage you did promise
This Lion?

PEWTER MAN AND LION
And the Scarecrow's brain?

WIZARD
Thou hast them all the while.

ALL TOGETHER
You forswear!

SCARECROW
You promised us things itself-- a real brain!

PEWTER MAN
A real heart!

LION
Real courage. That is what we wish.

WIZARD
It grieves me to here this.
Werefore ask not for flesh and blood?

SCARECROW and TINMAN
Can'st thou grant this?

WIZARD
Nay.
But any fool can have a brain. 'Tis a very common commodity.
Every craven creature that crawls pon land -- or
Slinks through slimy seas hath a brain!
From the rocky shores of Denmark to, well...
I defy the matter.
From whence I hail from, be there universities,

Where boys go to become learned men.
And upon their departure speak they three or four languages
Word for word without book,
And yet are altogether fool.
But they possess something you have not--
A degree!

Presents scroll to SCARECROW

Therefore, by virtue of the authority
Vested in me by the Universitatus
Committeeatum e plurbis unum, I hereby
Confer upon you the honorary degree of Philosopher.

SCARECROW
The more one sickens, the worse at ease he is.
Good pasture makes fat sheep.
He that hath learned no wit by nature nor art
May complain of good breeding or comes of a very dull kindred.
God's bodykins! I have a brain!
How can I thank thee?

WIZARD
Well, thou cans't.
(to LION)
Now, to you, my bestial friend,
Mistake not courage with wisdom.
From whence I came have we men the title hero
And on each Crispin's Day do they take
Their fortitude from dusty coffers and parade
Thru the streets Like great Pompy 'pon his return to Rome.
He writes brave verses, speaks brave words, swears brave
oaths, and breaks them bravely
Now, it is held that valour is the chiefest virtue, and

Most dignifies the haver: if it be,
The beast I speak of cannot in the world
Be singly counterpoised.

Hands LION a medal

Thou art the king of courage.
No man nor beast so potent breathes upon the ground
But I will beard him.

He kisses LION

LION
I am bereft of all words!

WIZARD (to PEWTER MAN)
As for thee, my armored cousin, wish you a heart?
Knowes't not how blessed thou art
To be without. For hearts shall nev'r be
Sensible till they be made unyielding.

The Sacred Heart

PEWTER MAN
But I am resolv'ed. To wreathe my arms,
Like a malecontent; to relish a love-song, like a
Robin-redbreast; to walk alone, like one that had
The pestilence; to sigh, like a school-boy that had
Lost his A B C; to weep, like a young wench that had
Buried her grandam; to fast, like one that takes
Diet; to watch like one that fears robbing; to

Speak puling, like a beggar at Hallowmas.

WIZARD
Where I hail from, are there men who do nothing
But good deeds.
And their hearts be no greater than yours.
Yet possess they something you have not: A testament.
Therefore, in consideration of thy kindness,
 I take most wondrous pleasure in presenting thee
With a bawble of our esteem and affection.
And remember, my sentimental knight,
That a heart be not judged by your love's depth,
But how much thou art belov'd by others.

PEWTER MAN
Hark! It ticks!

DOROTHY
Yes...!

LION
Read you what my medal says.
Courage! Be not the truth?

DOROTHY
Wondrous well!

SCARECROW (To Wizard)
But what of Dorothy?
PEWTER MAN
Ay, what of Dorothy?

LION
Ay.

WIZARD
Ah --

DOROTHY
I think there be no prize for me inside that purse.

WIZARD
What you will have, I'll give, and willing too;
For do we must what force will have us do.
Set on towards England, cousin, is it so?

DOROTHY
Oh, wilt thou? Be you a cunning enough Wizard?

WIZARD
Why child, I be an Englishman myself, bred and born not three hours' travel from Sussex.
Icarus the Flying Man, who with a troupe of wondrous entertainers did the country
Travel and enact miracles like flights of angels.
Until that time when bag of air did not return to ground.

LION
Say it so?

WIZARD
Verily. 'Twas I afloat in the heavens, a man without a country.

DOROTHY
Were you not afeard?

WIZARD
Afeard? Why, thou art speaking to he

Whom hath laughed in the visage of death,
Sneered at the edge of doom and crow'd at calamity
The fell of my hair did rouse and stir as life were in't.
And floating straight, obedient to the wind
Which was thrust forth of Kent,
Who most strangely upon this shore
Where you were wracked, was landed,
To be the lord on't.

DOROTHY
Oh!

WIZARD
As this unthought-on accident is guilty
To what we wildly do, so we profess
Ourselves to be the slaves of chance and flies
Of every wind that blows.
And on that wind, good Dorothy,
Shall we in haste return
To the blessed plot, the earth, the realm
The teeming womb of royal kings.

Enter CROWD with flying machine

Friends, Ozians, countrymen, lend me your ears!
I take my leave of you and 'tis our fast intent
To shake all cares and business from our age,
Conferring them on younger strengths while we
Unburdened crawl toward rest.
Good sir Scarecrow, by virtue of his wit, shall rule
Of all these bounds, even from this line to this,
With shadowy forests and with champains riched,
With plenteous rivers and wide-skirted meads,
With assist by the Man of Pewter by virtue of his heart

And Lion, by virtue of his courage.

CROWD cheers.

WIZARD
Our humble thanks.
(*To* SCARECROW)
Heavy is the head that wears the crown.

Exit cat pursued by TOTO

DOROTHY
Oh, come back again! Toto!
Come back! Oh, do not depart without me!
I shall return anon!
Oy! Toto!

The flying machine begins to rise

Design For A Flying Machine Drawing by Leonardo Da Vinci

PEWTER MAN
Seize the cur!

WIZARD
This be an irregular stratagem!
An absolutely untrod state.

PEWTER MAN
Oh! Help! He is hoisting sail!

WIZARD
-- Ravaged my exit!

PEWTER MAN
Help!

DOROTHY
Oh! Come back! Do not depart without me!
I beg thee, please come back again!

WIZARD
I cannot return for I know not how it performs!
Fare thee well good people of Oz!

CROWD
Fare thee well!

WIZARD
On heaven's breath I take my leave
But know within my heart I grieve!

Exit WIZARD

DOROTHY

All lost! Now I shall ne're return home!

LION
I pray thee, stay with us Dorothy. We all love thee and wish you
not leave.

DOROTHY
I wish I could find in my heart to stay here still,
But Oz is England not. My dearest Aunt must think me dead!
My good cuz, what shall I do?

SCARECROW
But look who comes here
One who may assist thee!

Enter GLINDA

DOROTHY
Oh, wilt thou help me? Cans't thou?

GLINDA
Thou art in no need of aid.
For the power to return home hath always been yours.

DOROTHY
Be it so?

SCARECROW
Wherefore did thee not reveal this urgent news?

GLINDA
She should not have believed me.
But to learn for own self.

PEWTER MAN
What hast thou learned my lady?

DOROTHY
Believe I 'twas not enough just to wish reunion with my Aunt
And Uncle--and if 'er I go searching for my heart's desire
Once 'gain, I shall look no further than mine own garden.
For if it be not there, 'twas never lost.
Be this true?

GLINDA
That is all.

SCARECROW
But 'tis so easy! I should have thought
of it for you.

PEWTER MAN
I should have felt the pangs in my heart.

GLINDA
Nay. 'Twas her own to discover.
Now, these bewitched shoes shall spirit thee home
Anon.

DOROTHY
Toto, too?

GLINDA
Toto, too.

DOROTHY
Presently?

GLINDA
Whenever you wish.

DOROTHY
O, parting is such sweet sorrow.
I would not wish
Any companions in the world but you,
Nor can imagination form a shape
Besides thyselves to like of.
(*to* PEWTER MAN)
Oh, good sir Knight of Pewter, weep no more.
Or you shall rust o'r again. Here be your balm.

PEWTER MAN
O, me! My heart, my rising heart! But, down!

Illustration by Jordan Monsell

DOROTHY
Fare thee well good Lion.
I shall miss your holler of help 'ere you found your courage.

LION
Ne'er would I have found it if not for thee.

DOROTHY (*to* SCARECROW)
I shall miss thee most of all
How many goodly creature are there here!
How beauteous Ozkind is! O brave new world,
That has such friends in't!

GLINDA
Be at the ready?

DOROTHY
Bid fare well, Toto.
I pray you all, know me when we meet again.
I wish you well, and so I take my leave.

GLINDA
Then shut thine eyes, and thrice tap thy heels.

DOROTHY *clicks heels together three times.*
GLINDA *waves wand.*

GLINDA
And think on this and nothing more
To be back home on distant shore--
There be no place like home;
There be no place like home...

DOROTHY
There be no place like home;
There be no place like home;
There be no place like home.   *(Blackout)*

ACT 5 scene 2

On deck of ship
Enter AUNT EM, Uncle HENRY, PROFESSOR, and
BOATSWAIN with DOROTHY

AUNT EM o.s.
Dorothy - Dorothy! It's me -- Aunt Em.
Awake.

DOROTHY
There be no place like home....there be no place like home...

AUNT EM
Dorothy. Dorothy, dear. It be your Aunt Em.

DOROTHY
Oh, good Aunt—it is you!

AUNT EM
Aye, child

Enter PROFESSOR

PROFESSOR
How fares the girl? A good knock o'er her
Coxcomb did she receive.
(to UNCLE HENRY)
By whose direction found'st thou out this ship?

UNCLE HENRY
By love, that first did prompt us to inquire.
He lent me counsel and I lent him eyes.
I am no pilot. Yet, wert she as far
As that vast shore washed with the farthest sea,

114

Shakespeare's Oz

I would adventure for such a child.

BOATSWAIN
And we are happy for it.
For with thy help, our ship—
Which, but three glasses since, we gave out split—
Is tight and yare and bravely rigged as when
We first put out to sea.

DOROTHY
I have had a most rare vision.

AUNT EM
Rest you now. You have had a dream—past the wit of man to
say what dream it was.

DOROTHY
But nay, a dream it was not.
The cloud-capped towers, the emerald palaces,
The great Oz itself—Yea, all which it inherit—did dissolve.
And leave not a rack behind.

AUNT EM
We are such stuff as dreams are made on, and our little life
Is rounded with a sleep.

DOROTHY
But 'twas real. And all I kept repeating was my desire to return
home.
Believe me not?

UNCLE HENRY
Certain we believe thee, Dorothy.

DOROTHY
But we are home, Toto! For it so falls out
That what we have we prize not to the worth
Whiles we enjoy it, but being lacked and lost,
Wherefore then we rack the value, then we find.
Enter CHORUS

Epilogue

CHORUS
Now my charms are all o'erthrown,
And what strength I have's mine own,
Which is most faint. Now, 'tis true,
I must be here confined by you.
To bedlam was our Dorothy sent
To shun these visions and repent
But she'd escape on floating bed
This world was not all in her head
Return to Oz would Dorothy go
For an encore of this show.
Now gentle breath of yours my sails
Must fill, or else my project fails,
Which was to please. Now I want
Spirits to enforce, art to enchant,
And my ending is despair,
Unless I be relieved by prayer,
Which pierces so that it assaults
Mercy itself and frees all faults.
As you from crimes would pardoned be,
Let your indulgence set me free.

116

The End

Shakespeare's Oz

AFTERWORD

In the year 1609, roughly one year before Shakespeare would write *The Tempest*, a small ship of English colonists bound for Virginia would be wrecked off the shores of Bermuda. A survivor, one William Strachey, would describe his ordeal in a letter, circulated back home. In his book *Shakespeare A-Z*, author Charles Boyce speculates that Shakespeare may have read Stracey's letter, and exploited it's accounts for *The Tempest*; specifically the shipwreck in 1.1, and Ariel's description of St. Elmo's Fire in 1.2.

But be it Bermuda or Virginia, Shakespeare was no doubt influenced by stories emerging from this new continent across the sea, just as author L. Frank Baum was influenced by the Bard's play of a wizard and his rule over an island of magical creatures. In fact, Baum frequently memorized passages of Shakespeare and even founded a Shakespearean troupe with his father's financial backing. Every great artist has stood on the shoulders of giants. Shakespeare had Chaucer and Plutarch; Baum had Carroll and Shakespeare.

The Wizard of Oz, first printed in 1900, almost 300 years after *The Tempest,* has become as iconic a piece of literature as any Shakespeare play. Schools and theatre companies across the globe continue to stage productions of both works, enchanting audiences of children and adults alike.

It was out of this enchantment for both authors that I have attempted to combine the two. Certainly, while *The Tempest* was the main source of inspiration, I used quotes from the entire Shakespeare canon, just as I used references from several of Baum's books, and not just the 1939 musical. For example, we do not learn of the Tinman's harrowing backstory in *The Wizard of Oz* but in the 1918 book *The Tin Woodman of Oz*. And when Dorothy first wakes upon the shores of Oz, it is Viola from *Twelfth Night* that she quotes.

I have no doubt that purists of Shakespeare and Baum will scoff at such an adaptation. But it is my hope that if you are holding this book that the words within have renewed your interest in these authors, and that a Caliban quoting Cowardly Lion made you smile and forget about your troubles if only for a brief moment.

Jordan Monsell
Los Angeles, California

Acknowledgements

I'd like to thank my friends Drina Krieger, David Topf, and Bryan Mahoney for their wise suggestions, the LA weekly and Daily Ozmapolitan for their kind reviews, the helpful staff of the Los Angeles Central Library, and above all, L. Frank Baum and William Shakespeare.

About the Author

Jordan Monsell is the author and cover artist of *Ministers of Grace: The Unauthorized Shakespearean Parody of Ghostbusters.* He received his BFA in Theatre from The University of Connecticut in 2001 and now resides in Los Angeles with his cat Sir Percival. *Shakespeare's Oz* is his second book. Follow him on Instagram @jmonsell

Praise for *Ministers of Grace: The Unauthorized Shakespearean Parody of Ghostbusters*

"Absolutely Hilarious"
~ *Nerdist*

"Monsell has trance channeled the Bard in genuine, scholarly and hilarious fashion"
~*Dan Aykroyd*

"I legit laughed, and laughed pretty darn hard."
~Ghostbusters News

"A smart, intelligently crafted, and wickedly funny mash-up joyride."
~Shakespeare in LA

Available on Amazon.com

Made in the USA
Columbia, SC
01 September 2021